Silent Echoes

Silent Echoes

Michelle Hartman

Table of Contents

Prologue

The night was eerily silent, save for the occasional rustle of leaves in the gentle breeze. The town of Silver Creek lay nestled in the valley, its residents blissfully unaware of the impending event that would shatter their tranquility. The sky above, a canvas of inky black dotted with shimmering stars, seemed to pulse with an otherworldly energy.

It began with a faint hum, barely perceptible at first, but growing steadily louder. The animals in the surrounding farms grew restless, their instinctual fear sensing the unnatural presence. In the distance, a solitary light appeared, hovering above the horizon. It moved with a fluidity that defied the laws of physics, casting an eerie glow over the landscape.

John, a seasoned farmer with a pragmatic outlook on life, stood on his porch, his weathered face etched with concern. He watched as the light grew brighter, its movements erratic yet purposeful. As it drew closer, the hum intensified, resonating deep within his bones. John's heart raced, a mixture of fear and curiosity propelling him forward.

He stepped off the porch, his eyes locked on the inexplicable phenomenon above. The light descended slowly, illuminating the fields in an ethereal glow. John's breath caught in his throat as he realized this was no ordinary aircraft. It was something far beyond human comprehension.

Without warning, the light engulfed him, blinding and all-encompassing. John felt a strange sensation, as if his very essence was being pulled from his body. Panic surged through him, but before he could react, everything went black.

The town of Silver Creek remained oblivious to John's fate. The light vanished as quickly as it had appeared, leaving no trace of its presence. The only evidence of the encounter was a lingering silence, an unsettling echo of the extraordinary event.

Unbeknownst to the townspeople, this was just the beginning. The silent echoes would soon reverberate through their lives, unraveling the fabric of their reality and revealing a truth that lay hidden in the vast expanse of the cosmos.

Chapter 1

The Ordinary Day

Dr. Emily Harper loved the serenity of early mornings at the Silver Creek Observatory. The air was crisp, the sky a pale shade of dawn, and the world seemed to hold its breath in anticipation of the day. She sat in her office, sipping a steaming cup of coffee, her eyes scanning the latest data from last night's observation.

Emily was in her mid-thirties, with sharp green eyes and a mane of auburn hair that she often tied back in a loose ponytail. Her dedication to her work had earned her a reputation as one of the leading astronomers in the country. Yet, despite her achievements, she was always searching, always questioning. The universe held too many secrets for her to rest easy.

"Morning, Dr. Harper," came a cheerful voice from the doorway. It was Sarah, her ten-year-old daughter, with a bright smile that lit up the room. "Did you find any aliens last night?"

Emily chuckled, ruffling Sarah's hair as she set her coffee down. "Not last night, but who knows what today might bring?"

Sarah was the light of Emily's life. Her inquisitive nature and boundless energy were constant reminders of the wonders of childhood. They had a special bond, strengthened by their mutual love for the stars. Sarah often joined her mother at the observatory, asking endless questions and dreaming of exploring the cosmos.

After dropping Sarah off at school, Emily headed back to the observatory. Her colleagues were already at work, analyzing data and preparing for the upcoming night of stargazing. She settled into her office, immersing herself in the patterns and anomalies that danced across her computer screen.

The day passed in a blur of calculations and meetings. By evening, Emily felt the familiar excitement that came with the onset of night. As the sky darkened, the observatory's dome began to open, revealing the vast expanse of the universe.

"Everything looks good, Emily," said Jake, her research assistant, as he adjusted the telescope. "Clear skies tonight."

"Perfect," Emily replied, her eyes twinkling with anticipation. "Let's see what we can find."

Hours passed as they scanned the heavens, capturing images of distant galaxies and charting the movement of celestial bodies. Emily was lost in her work, her mind swimming with the infinite possibilities of the universe.

It was just after midnight when she noticed something unusual. A series of lights, moving in a pattern that defied explanation, appeared on the monitor. Emily leaned closer, her heart pounding with excitement and a hint of apprehension.

"Jake, look at this," she called out.

Jake hurried over, his eyes widening as he studied the screen. "That's... not a satellite, is it?"

"No," Emily replied, her voice barely a whisper. "It's something else."

The lights moved in a deliberate, almost intelligent manner. Emily's fingers flew over the keyboard, capturing as much data as possible.

She felt a chill run down her spine as the realization dawned on her—this was no ordinary astronomical event.

The lights suddenly vanished, leaving Emily and Jake staring at a blank screen. They exchanged glances, the gravity of the situation sinking in.

"We need to report this," Jake said, his voice trembling slightly.

Emily nodded, already composing an email to her superiors. As she typed, her mind raced with questions. What had they just witnessed? Was it a natural phenomenon, or something more extraordinary?

As the night wore on, Emily couldn't shake the feeling that her life was about to change in ways she couldn't yet comprehend. The ordinary day had given way to an extraordinary night, and the mysteries of the universe seemed closer than ever before

Chapter 2

The First Encounter

John Michaels had always been a man of the land. His farm, passed down through generations, was his pride and joy. He knew every inch of his property, from the rolling pastures to the dense woods at the edge. But tonight, as he stood on his porch, the familiar landscape seemed alien and foreboding.

The humming sound had returned, louder and more insistent than before. John squinted into the darkness, trying to make sense of the strange lights that danced above his fields. He felt an unease he couldn't explain, a primal fear that gripped his heart.

Grabbing a flashlight, he descended the steps of his porch and walked toward the source of the disturbance. The beam of his flashlight cut through the night, but it did little to dispel the growing sense of dread. As he approached the fields, the lights grew brighter, casting an eerie glow over the crops.

"Who's out there?" John called out, his voice trembling. "Show yourself!"

There was no response, only the persistent hum that seemed to vibrate through his very bones. He took a few more steps, his eyes locked on the lights. They hovered in the air, pulsating with a rhythm that seemed almost alive.

Suddenly, the lights shifted, converging into a single, blinding beam that enveloped John. He felt a strange sensation, as if his body was weightless, suspended in a void. Panic surged through him, but his limbs refused to obey his commands. He was frozen, caught in the grip of an unseen force.

As quickly as it began, the light vanished. John found himself lying in the middle of his field, gasping for breath. His flashlight was gone, and the hum had ceased, leaving only the deafening silence of the night.

Shaking, he struggled to his feet and stumbled back to the farmhouse. He locked the doors, his mind racing with questions. What had he just experienced? Had it been a dream, or something far more sinister?

The next morning, John awoke to find strange marks on his body—small, circular burns that he couldn't explain. He tried to convince himself it was all a bad dream, but the evidence was there, etched into his skin.

Determined to find answers, he drove into town to speak with the local authorities. Sheriff Thompson listened patiently, but his skeptical expression told John all he needed to know.

"Look, John," the sheriff said, leaning back in his chair. "We've had a few reports of strange lights lately, but nothing concrete. Probably just some kids playing with drones or something."

John shook his head. "This was no drone, Sheriff. I know what I saw. And these marks—" He pulled up his sleeve to reveal the burns. "—they weren't there before."

The sheriff sighed. "I'll make a note of it, but there's not much we can do without more evidence."

Frustrated, John left the station, feeling more isolated than ever. He knew what he had experienced was real, but without proof, no one would believe him. As he drove back to the farm, he couldn't shake the feeling that he was being watched.

Meanwhile, at the Silver Creek Observatory, Emily was grappling with her own set of questions. The mysterious lights she had observed the previous night had left her shaken. She spent hours analyzing the data, trying to find a logical explanation, but the patterns defied all known scientific principles.

Emily decided to visit John, having heard about his encounter through the town's grapevine. She hoped that his experience might shed some light on the phenomenon she had witnessed.

When she arrived at the farm, John was reluctant to talk at first. But Emily's genuine curiosity and professional demeanor eventually won him over. He recounted his experience in detail, showing her the marks on his body.

Emily listened intently, her mind racing with possibilities. Could there be a connection between the lights and John's encounter? She decided to take a closer look at the field where John had seen the lights.

As they walked through the field, Emily's eyes scanned the ground for any signs of disturbance. She noticed strange, circular impressions in the soil, as if something heavy had pressed down into the earth. She took samples for analysis, hoping they might provide some answers.

Back at the observatory, Emily examined the soil samples under a microscope. What she found was both fascinating and disturbing— traces of an unknown substance that emitted a faint, otherworldly glow. It was unlike anything she had ever seen before.

Determined to get to the bottom of the mystery, Emily contacted Mark, the local journalist known for his investigations into UFO sightings. She shared her findings with him, and together they began to piece together the puzzle.

As they delved deeper, they uncovered a pattern of disappearances and strange phenomena that stretched back decades. The pieces of the puzzle were falling into place, but the picture they formed was more terrifying than they could have imagined.

Emily knew she was on the brink of a groundbreaking discovery, but she also knew the dangers that came with it. The ordinary day had given way to an extraordinary journey, one that would test her resolve and push the boundaries of her understanding.

Chapter 3

Disappearances

The town of Silver Creek was gripped by a growing sense of unease. The strange lights in the sky, the mysterious burns on John's body, and the eerie hum that had been reported by several residents—all pointed to something beyond the realm of the ordinary. Rumors spread like wildfire, and fear took root in the hearts of the townspeople.

Sarah Harper sat in her classroom, staring out the window. Her best friend, Lisa, hadn't shown up for school that day. It wasn't like Lisa to skip class, especially not without telling her. Sarah tried to focus on the lesson, but her mind kept drifting to the strange stories she'd overheard. She couldn't shake the feeling that something was terribly wrong.

At lunchtime, Sarah decided to visit Lisa's house. She hoped that maybe Lisa was just sick and hadn't been able to call. But when she arrived, Lisa's mother greeted her with a worried expression.

"Sarah, have you seen Lisa?" Mrs. Johnson asked, her voice trembling.

"No, I was hoping she was here," Sarah replied, her heart sinking.

Mrs. Johnson's eyes filled with tears. "She never came home last night. We called the police, but they haven't found anything."

Fear gripped Sarah. She promised Mrs. Johnson she would help look for Lisa, but deep down, she feared the worst. As she walked back to the observatory, her mind raced with thoughts of her friend's fate.

Meanwhile, Emily was engrossed in her research. She and Mark had been working tirelessly, compiling evidence and trying to make sense of the strange occurrences. The soil samples from John's field had revealed more than just the unknown substance—they also contained traces of radiation, unlike anything found on Earth.

"Emily, you need to see this," Mark said, bursting into her office with a stack of papers. "I've been digging through old newspaper archives. Look at these."

He spread the papers across her desk, revealing headlines that spanned decades. Each article detailed unexplained disappearances, strange lights, and government cover-ups. The pattern was undeniable —Silver Creek had been a hotspot for unexplained phenomena for years.

Emily's eyes widened as she read through the articles. "How did we miss this? Why hasn't anyone connected the dots before?"

"Because it's been buried," Mark replied grimly. "Someone doesn't want the truth to come out. But we're getting closer."

Their conversation was interrupted by a knock on the door. It was Sarah, her face pale and eyes wide with fear.

"Mom, Lisa's missing," she said, her voice trembling. "She never came home last night."

Emily's heart sank. She hugged Sarah tightly, trying to reassure her even as her own mind raced with worry. "We'll find her, Sarah. I promise."

As Emily comforted her daughter, Mark's phone buzzed with a new message. He glanced at the screen and his expression grew serious.

"Emily, we need to go," he said urgently. "Another sighting was reported near the old mill. We might find some answers there."

Emily nodded, kissing Sarah's forehead. "Stay here with Jake, okay? I'll be back soon."

With Mark leading the way, they drove to the outskirts of town. The old mill had been abandoned for years, but it was now at the center of their investigation. As they approached, the familiar hum filled the air, growing louder with each step.

They reached the clearing around the mill and saw the lights—bright, pulsating orbs that hovered above the ground. Emily's heart pounded as she and Mark crept closer, trying to stay hidden.

Suddenly, the lights shifted, converging into a single beam that illuminated the area around them. Emily gasped as she saw figures emerging from the light—humanoid, but not human. They moved with a fluid grace, their features obscured by the blinding glow.

Mark reached for his camera, snapping photos as quickly as he could. The figures seemed to notice them, turning their attention toward the intruders. The hum intensified, and Emily felt a strange sensation, like a tugging at the edges of her consciousness.

"Emily, we need to go," Mark whispered urgently, grabbing her arm.

But Emily was rooted to the spot, unable to tear her eyes away from the sight. One of the figures stepped forward, its eyes locking onto hers. In that moment, she felt a connection—a flood of images and emotions that overwhelmed her senses.

She saw flashes of distant worlds, advanced technology, and a deep, ancient sorrow. The images faded as quickly as they had come, leaving her breathless and disoriented.

Mark tugged her arm again, pulling her back to reality. "Emily, now!"

They ran back to the car, the lights behind them fading into the night. As they sped away, Emily's mind raced with the implications of what she'd seen. The figures, the connection—everything pointed to something far beyond their understanding.

Back at the observatory, Emily and Mark reviewed the photos and data they'd collected. The evidence was undeniable, but it also raised more questions than answers.

"What did you see out there?" Mark asked, his voice filled with awe and curiosity.

Emily took a deep breath, trying to articulate the experience. "I don't know, Mark. But whatever it is, it's intelligent. And it's been watching us for a long time."

As they continued their investigation, the pieces of the puzzle slowly began to fall into place. But the more they uncovered, the more they realized just how dangerous their quest for the truth had become.

Chapter 4

The Investigation

The days following the sighting at the old mill were a whirlwind of activity for Emily and Mark. The photographs and data they had collected provided compelling evidence, but they needed more to understand the full scope of what was happening in Silver Creek.

Emily sat in her office, staring at the images on her computer screen. The figures they had seen were unlike anything she had ever encountered. She knew that revealing this information to the public would cause panic, but she also felt a responsibility to uncover the truth.

"Emily, we need to be careful," Mark said, breaking the silence. "If the government has been covering this up for years, they'll do anything to keep it that way."

"I know," Emily replied, rubbing her temples. "But we can't stop now. Too many people have been affected, and we need to find Lisa."

Mark nodded, his expression resolute. "Let's start with the people who have experienced these phenomena firsthand. Maybe their stories will give us more clues."

They spent the next few days interviewing townspeople who had reported sightings or strange encounters. Each story added a new piece to the puzzle, painting a picture of an ongoing, systematic series of abductions and unexplained events.

One evening, as they were going through their notes, Emily received a call from a woman named Alice Thompson. Alice claimed to have information about the disappearances and wanted to meet in person. They arranged to meet at a secluded café on the outskirts of town.

Alice was already waiting when they arrived, nervously sipping a cup of coffee. She was in her late forties, with a tired, haunted look in her eyes.

"Thank you for meeting with us," Emily said, sitting down across from her. "You said you have information about the disappearances?"

Alice nodded, glancing around to make sure they weren't being overheard. "I've seen them," she whispered. "The lights, the figures. They took my husband five years ago. I never told anyone because I knew they wouldn't believe me."

Emily and Mark exchanged a glance. "Can you tell us what happened?" Mark asked gently.

Alice took a deep breath, her hands trembling. "It was late at night. We were out on the porch, enjoying the stars. Suddenly, the lights appeared, just like you described. They were so bright, I could barely see. My husband went to investigate, and then he was just... gone. I tried to run, but something held me in place. I felt like I was floating, like my mind was being pulled apart."

She paused, tears streaming down her face. "When I woke up, I was alone. I searched for him, but there was no trace. The authorities dismissed it as a runaway case, but I know what I saw."

Emily reached out, squeezing Alice's hand. "I'm so sorry, Alice. Thank you for sharing your story. We'll do everything we can to find out what's happening."

As they left the café, Emily and Mark felt a renewed sense of urgency. They were getting closer to the truth, but the danger was also growing. They decided to dig deeper into the government cover-up, hoping to find a lead that would break the case wide open.

Their investigation led them to a retired military officer named Colonel Robert Hayes. He had been involved in a top-secret project decades ago and had since become a recluse. After several attempts to contact him, they finally received a cryptic message agreeing to a meeting.

The rendezvous took place in an abandoned warehouse on the outskirts of town. Colonel Hayes was a stern, weathered man with a piercing gaze that seemed to see right through them.

"I know why you're here," he said without preamble. "And I have to warn you—you're treading on dangerous ground."

"We're not here to cause trouble," Emily said. "We just want the truth. People are disappearing, and we need to know why."

The colonel sighed, running a hand through his graying hair. "The truth is, there are things out there—things we don't understand. The project I was part of was meant to study these phenomena, but it quickly became clear that we were in over our heads. We made contact, but it came at a cost. People started disappearing, just like you said. The government decided it was safer to cover it up than to risk a public panic."

"Why didn't you come forward?" Mark asked.

"Because they threatened my family," Hayes replied, his voice heavy with regret. "But now, seeing what's happening, I can't stay silent anymore. I have documents, evidence of the project's existence and the government's involvement. It's all hidden in a safe place. I'll give it to you, but you have to promise me you'll be careful. They won't hesitate to silence anyone who gets too close."

Emily and Mark promised to protect Hayes and his family, and in return, he handed over a key and directions to a remote storage unit. As they left the warehouse, they knew they were holding the key to unraveling the entire mystery.

Chapter 5

Abducted

Emily and Mark drove to the remote storage unit with a sense of urgency. The key that Colonel Hayes had given them felt heavy in Emily's pocket, a tangible reminder of the responsibility they now bore. The storage unit was located in a secluded area on the outskirts of town, surrounded by overgrown vegetation and rusted chain-link fences.

As they approached the unit, Emily's heart raced with anticipation. She inserted the key into the lock, her hands trembling slightly. The door creaked open, revealing a dimly lit space filled with dusty boxes and old military equipment. Mark switched on a flashlight, illuminating the interior as they began their search.

It didn't take long for them to find the documents. Tucked away in a weathered briefcase, the files were marked with government seals and classified stamps. Emily carefully opened the briefcase, revealing a trove of information that detailed the top-secret project Colonel Hayes had mentioned.

They spent hours pouring over the documents, which included photographs, transcripts of communications, and detailed reports of the encounters. The evidence was overwhelming, painting a chilling picture of a covert operation that had been monitoring and interacting with extraterrestrial beings for decades.

"This is incredible," Mark said, his voice filled with awe. "We have to get this out to the public. People need to know the truth."

Emily nodded, her mind racing with thoughts of how to safely disseminate the information. But as they discussed their next steps, a sudden noise outside the storage unit startled them. The hum they had come to dread filled the air, growing louder and more intense.

"Mark, do you hear that?" Emily whispered, her heart pounding.

Before he could respond, the unit was flooded with a blinding light. Emily felt the familiar sensation of weightlessness, her body lifting off the ground as if pulled by an invisible force. She tried to scream, but no sound escaped her lips. The light engulfed them both, and everything went black.

When Emily regained consciousness, she found herself in a sterile, dimly lit room. The walls were smooth and metallic, and a soft, pulsing light emanated from the ceiling. She tried to move, but her limbs felt heavy and unresponsive.

"Mark?" she called out, her voice echoing in the confined space.

"Emily, over here," came Mark's voice from somewhere to her left. She turned her head and saw him lying on a similar metallic surface, his eyes wide with fear.

"Where are we?" Emily asked, struggling to sit up.

"I think we're on their ship," Mark replied, his voice trembling. "We were abducted."

Emily's mind raced as she tried to process their situation. The room was eerily quiet, save for the rhythmic pulsing of the light. She took a deep breath, trying to calm her racing heart. They needed to find a way out, to escape and warn the others.

As they looked around, a door slid open with a soft hiss, and a figure stepped into the room. It was one of the beings they had seen at the old mill, its form slender and ethereal, with large, dark eyes that seemed to pierce through their very souls.

Emily felt a strange sense of calm wash over her, as if the being was projecting emotions directly into her mind. It approached her, its movements graceful and fluid, and placed a hand on her forehead. A flood of images and sensations overwhelmed her senses—a vast, starry expanse, advanced technology, and a deep, abiding sorrow.

She realized that the beings were not hostile, but rather seeking help. They had been observing humanity for centuries, trying to find a way to communicate. The abductions were a desperate attempt to understand and prevent a catastrophe that threatened both their world and ours.

Emily's mind reeled with the implications. She and Mark had to find a way to convey this information to the world, to bridge the gap between their species and ours. But first, they needed to escape.

The being seemed to understand her thoughts. It released her and stepped back, allowing her to regain her composure. Emily looked at Mark, who nodded in silent agreement. They had to take this chance.

"Thank you," Emily said, her voice steady. "We understand now. We will help you, but we need to return to our world to do so."

The being tilted its head, as if considering her words. It then gestured toward the door, indicating that they should follow. Emily and Mark exchanged a hopeful glance and followed the being through the ship's corridors.

They passed other rooms filled with strange devices and more of the ethereal beings, all working in silent coordination. Eventually, they reached a chamber with a large, circular portal that shimmered with a soft, blue light.

The being gestured for them to step through. Emily took a deep breath and held Mark's hand as they walked into the light. The sensation of weightlessness returned, and the world around them dissolved into a blur of colors and shapes.

When they opened their eyes, they found themselves back in the storage unit, the documents scattered around them. The hum was gone, replaced by the familiar sounds of the world outside. They had returned.

Emily and Mark knew they had to act quickly. They gathered the documents and made their way back to the observatory, their minds filled with the knowledge and the urgency of their mission. The truth was out there, and they were determined to reveal it, to bridge the gap between humanity and the beings that had been watching them for so long.

Chapter 6

The Escape

Back at the observatory, Emily and Mark wasted no time organizing their findings. They knew that revealing the truth would not be easy. The documents provided by Colonel Hayes were crucial, but they needed to ensure their safety and verify their claims before making any public announcements.

"We need to make multiple copies of these documents," Mark suggested, "and distribute them to trusted contacts. That way, if something happens to us, the information will still get out."

Emily agreed. They spent the next several hours scanning the documents and encrypting digital copies. They sent these to colleagues in various fields—journalists, scientists, and even a few sympathetic government officials. Each message included a detailed explanation of their findings and a plea for help.

As the sun began to rise, casting a golden hue over the observatory, Emily felt a renewed sense of hope. They were not alone in this fight. With the evidence now distributed, they could focus on finding Lisa and uncovering more about the beings' intentions.

Just as they were about to take a break, Emily's phone buzzed with a message. It was from an anonymous source, claiming to have information about the government cover-up and the location of other abductees. The message included coordinates to a remote facility in the mountains.

"This could be a trap," Mark warned, looking over Emily's shoulder.

"I know," Emily replied, "but it's a risk we have to take. If there's a chance we can find Lisa and others like her, we need to follow this lead."

They packed their gear and set out for the mountains, their minds racing with possibilities. The journey was long and treacherous, the winding roads and dense forests adding to the tension.

As they approached the coordinates, they saw a heavily guarded compound nestled in a secluded valley. High fences, surveillance cameras, and armed guards made it clear that this was no ordinary facility.

"We need a plan," Mark said, studying the layout through binoculars. "We can't just walk in there."

Emily nodded. "We need a distraction. If we can create enough chaos, we might be able to slip inside and find the abductees."

They scouted the perimeter, looking for a weak point in the security. Finally, they found an area where the fence was less fortified, hidden by thick underbrush. They decided to set a small fire as a diversion, hoping to draw the guards away from the main entrance.

As the fire took hold, alarms blared, and the guards scrambled to contain the blaze. Emily and Mark seized the opportunity, slipping through the fence and making their way toward the main building. They moved quickly and quietly, their hearts pounding with adrenaline.

Inside, the facility was a maze of corridors and locked doors. They navigated carefully, using a stolen keycard to access restricted areas. Finally, they reached a large, dimly lit room filled with holding cells.

Inside, they saw people—men, women, and children—huddled together, their eyes filled with fear and exhaustion.

"Lisa!" Emily called out, her voice echoing through the room.

A small figure stepped forward, her face pale and gaunt but unmistakably Lisa. "Dr. Harper?" she whispered, tears welling up in her eyes.

Emily rushed to the cell, her hands shaking as she tried to unlock the door. "We're getting you out of here," she promised.

As they freed the abductees, Emily and Mark realized the magnitude of their task. There were too many to escape unnoticed. They needed to find another way out.

"There's a loading dock at the back," one of the captives said. "I overheard the guards talking about it. It's not as heavily guarded."

With the captives' help, they made their way to the loading dock. The guards were still preoccupied with the fire, giving them a narrow window of opportunity. They loaded everyone into an abandoned truck and drove away from the facility, their hearts pounding with relief and fear.

As they sped down the mountain roads, Emily glanced at the faces of the rescued captives. Each one carried a story of terror and resilience, and each one was a testament to the urgency of their mission.

They returned to Silver Creek, where they were met by a group of journalists and allies. The rescued captives' stories, combined with the documents, painted a damning picture of the government's involvement in the cover-up.

Emily and Mark knew that this was just the beginning. The battle for the truth was far from over, but they were no longer alone. With the support of the community and the world watching, they had a chance to expose the truth and protect humanity from the unknown.

Chapter 7

The Truth Revealed

The town hall of Silver Creek was filled to capacity. Journalists, townspeople, and curious onlookers packed the room, their faces a mix of anticipation and anxiety. The air buzzed with murmurs as Emily and Mark prepared to present their findings. The rescued abductees sat in the front row, their presence lending weight to the gravity of the situation.

Emily stepped up to the podium, her heart pounding. She took a deep breath, steadying herself before addressing the crowd.

"Thank you all for coming," she began. "What we are about to reveal may be difficult to believe, but I assure you, it is the truth. For years, our town—and many others—have been the sites of unexplained phenomena, abductions, and government cover-ups. Today, we have the evidence to prove it."

She gestured to a screen behind her, where images and documents began to display. The photographs of the strange lights, the figures, and the documents detailing the top-secret project were projected for everyone to see.

Mark took over, explaining the connection between the sightings, the disappearances, and the government's involvement. He detailed their encounters, the evidence they had gathered, and the testimonies of the abductees.

As they spoke, the room grew silent, the weight of the revelations sinking in. When they finished, the room erupted in a flurry of questions and exclamations.

"How long has this been going on?" one journalist asked.

"Decades," Emily replied. "The documents date back to the mid-20th century. This has been happening under our noses for far too long."

"What do the aliens want?" another person asked, their voice trembling with fear.

Emily paused, choosing her words carefully. "The beings we encountered are not hostile. They have been trying to communicate with us, to warn us of a catastrophe that threatens both our worlds. Their methods may seem frightening, but their intentions are not malevolent."

The crowd murmured, processing this information. Emily could see the fear and skepticism in their eyes, but also a glimmer of hope.

As the meeting continued, a group of government officials arrived, led by a stern-looking man in a dark suit. He approached the podium, his expression unreadable.

"Dr. Harper, Mr. Anderson," he said, addressing Emily and Mark. "I am Agent Roberts from the Department of Defense. We need to speak with you immediately."

Emily and Mark exchanged a glance, knowing this confrontation was inevitable. They followed Agent Roberts into a private room, where he closed the door behind them.

"You've caused quite a stir," Roberts said, his tone calm but authoritative. "The information you've revealed is highly classified. You must understand the ramifications of your actions."

"We understand perfectly," Emily replied, her voice steady. "But the truth needs to come out. People deserve to know what's happening."

Roberts sighed, rubbing his temples. "You're right. The government has kept this under wraps for too long. But releasing this information publicly is dangerous. It could cause mass panic and disrupt national security."

"People are already panicking," Mark interjected. "Keeping them in the dark isn't helping. We need transparency and cooperation if we're going to address this threat."

Roberts studied them for a moment before nodding. "Very well. We'll cooperate. But you need to understand that this is a delicate situation. We'll need to work together to manage the fallout and ensure the safety of everyone involved."

Over the next few weeks, a task force was formed, comprising government officials, scientists, and representatives from the community. They worked tirelessly to develop a plan for communication and cooperation with the extraterrestrial beings.

Emily and Mark continued their research, now with the full support of the government. They focused on understanding the technology and motives of the beings, seeking ways to prevent the impending catastrophe.

The abductees, including Lisa, received medical care and psychological support. Their testimonies were recorded and analyzed, providing valuable insights into the nature of the encounters.

As the months passed, progress was made. A communication protocol was established with the beings, allowing for a more direct and peaceful exchange of information. The public was gradually informed about the situation, with efforts made to educate and reassure them.

Silver Creek became a hub of scientific and diplomatic activity, a symbol of hope and cooperation in the face of an unprecedented challenge. Emily and Mark's relentless pursuit of the truth had paved the way for a new era of understanding and collaboration.

In the end, the mystery of the silent echoes in the sky was unraveled, revealing a story of connection and resilience. Humanity had taken its first steps into a larger universe, ready to face the unknown with courage and unity.

Epilogue

The sun set over Silver Creek, casting a warm, golden glow over the town that had become a symbol of hope and resilience. The once-quiet town was now bustling with activity, a center of scientific research and diplomatic efforts that spanned the globe—and beyond.

Dr. Emily Harper stood on the balcony of the newly established Silver Creek Research Center, gazing up at the stars. It had been a year since the revelations that had changed her life, and the lives of everyone in the town. The world had been forever altered by the knowledge of extraterrestrial beings and the impending catastrophe that had united humanity in a common cause.

The research center was a testament to human ingenuity and collaboration. Scientists from around the world worked together to develop new technologies, understand the advanced alien science, and prepare for the challenges that lay ahead. Communication with the extraterrestrial beings had improved, leading to a deeper understanding of their motives and the shared threats facing both worlds.

Emily took a deep breath, savoring the cool evening air. She had come a long way from the solitary nights at the observatory, scanning the skies for answers. Now, she was at the forefront of a global effort to secure a future for humanity.

"Mom?" came a voice from behind her.

Emily turned to see her daughter, Sarah, standing in the doorway. The past year had been difficult for Sarah, but she had shown incredible strength and resilience. She had been reunited with her friend Lisa, and together, they had become symbols of hope for the abductees who had returned.

"Hey, sweetie," Emily said, smiling. "What are you doing up here?"

Sarah walked over to the balcony, her eyes reflecting the same curiosity and wonder that had always driven her mother. "I was just thinking about everything that's happened. Do you think we're really safe now?"

Emily put an arm around her daughter's shoulders, pulling her close. "We've come a long way, and there's still a lot of work to be done. But we've learned so much, and we're not alone in this. We have allies— both here on Earth and out there in the stars."

Sarah nodded, looking up at the night sky. "Do you think we'll ever get to visit their world?"

"Maybe someday," Emily replied, her gaze following Sarah's. "For now, we need to focus on taking care of our own world and making sure we're ready for whatever comes next."

As they stood together, the stars seemed to shine a little brighter, a reminder of the vastness of the universe and the endless possibilities that lay ahead.

In the distance, the lights of the research center flickered, a beacon of hope in the darkness. Emily knew that the road ahead would be challenging, but she was confident that humanity was ready to face it. With the knowledge they had gained and the partnerships they had forged, they were prepared to confront the unknown and build a future where Earth and its new allies could thrive together.

As the first stars of the evening appeared, Emily whispered a silent promise to herself and to the beings that had reached out to them: they would not let fear divide them. Instead, they would embrace the unknown with courage and unity, ready to explore the mysteries of the universe and protect their shared home.

And so, under the silent echoes of the night sky, Silver Creek stood as a testament to the power of discovery, the strength of human spirit, and the hope for a brighter tomorrow.